MISTLETOE KISSES

SHAW HART

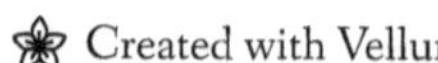 Created with Vellum

BLURB

Mason has been in love with his assistant, Noel, since he hired her. She's the first woman to get his attention and the only one that he wants to make his.

There's only one problem. He's afraid that his dark tastes will scare his sweet assistant away.

Noel has always had a crush on her boss but she's never acted on it. She can't without risking losing her job. When Mason kisses her under the mistletoe though, she wonders if maybe it wouldn't be much of a risk after all.

Will a kiss under the office mistletoe lead these two to their happily ever after?

ONE

Mason

SHE'S WEARING that damn skirt again.

I scowl through the floor to ceiling glass wall as she bends over her desk, her round ass sticking up in the air and taunting me. The snug black material clings to her curves and has my cock ready to burst out of my suit pants.

I swear to god, she does it on purpose.

My hand slips beneath my wood desk, pressing down on my cock as I struggle to tear my eyes away from the scene just out front of my office. My dick jerks against my hand, urging me to stand from my desk, drag her in here, and turn the frosted glass on so no one can see me bend her over every available surface on my desk as I fuck her raw.

"Fuck," I hiss as I jerk away from my desk and stalk into the bathroom attached to my office.

I've been spending more and more time in this bathroom since I hired Noel four months ago to be my assistant. She probably thinks that there's something wrong with me, but the truth is that I can't seem to go more than a few hours in her presence without having to take myself in hand.

I glare at my reflection in the mirror above the sink as I hurry to unbuckle my belt and take my cock out. I fist myself roughly, groaning as my eyes fall closed and I picture my curvy little assistant on her knees before me.

Her mouth is open wide, her tongue out and licking the tip of me as my hand works my length.

"Let me do it," she whispers, her eyes mischievous emeralds as she wraps her tiny hand around me.

My head dips back, my throat working hard as she wraps her lips around me and sucks. Her hand is—

"Mr. Roth?" Noel asks tentatively from right outside the door and I bite back a groan.

My hand tightens around my length and I stroke myself faster.

"Yes?" I choke out as I picture her in here with me, her big eyes looking up at me as I balance her on the edge of the counter and slip between her creamy thighs.

In my fantasies, she spreads her legs wider, urging me to take her harder, deeper. Her hair is mussed from my fingers, her lips swollen and red from sucking my cock. Her mouth opens and she pleads with me to come inside her —"

"Can I get you anything?" Noel asks from outside the door and I imagine asking her to come in here and take care of this hard on.

Imagining her slipping inside the bathroom with a sly smile has me biting back a growl as I spill into my hand. I lean against the counter, trying to catch my breath discreetly as I hear Noel shift outside the door.

"Coffee," I bark and I hear her scurry off to grab me my usual.

I shouldn't be such an asshole to her but I can't seem to

help myself. I'm always so tense around her, afraid that I'm just going to reach out and grab her. I'd have her underneath me or pinned to the nearest surface before I could stop myself.

I clean up, splashing some cold water on my face before I tuck myself back into my slacks and head back into my office.

Noel is just coming back into my office with a cup of coffee and some kind of pastry on a small plate.

"Brenda brought in some cookies! They're delicious and I snagged you one," she says with a bright smile and I curl my fingers into my palm, drawing on all of my strength to not pull her down into my lap.

Her golden hair glows under the lights as she sets the coffee cup down in front of me and then slides the cookie closer to me. I eye the treat like it will bite me and Noel uses her index finger to push it even closer to me. I look up into her shining eyes and even though I don't want the cookie, I find myself picking it up and taking a bite of it.

"So good, right?" She asks with a smile that has me finishing the rest of the cookie.

I barely taste it, too focused on taking in the goddess in front of me. Her red button up shirt is tucked into the waistband of that tight black skirt that I both love and really fucking hate. The buttons are straining over her tits and for one second I wish that they would pop, letting me see the black lace bra that I caught a peek of when she bent over to put the coffee and cookie down.

It doesn't and I sigh.

"Thanks," I mumble.

"You are so welcome," she says with the brightest smile. "So, I've got your schedule organized for the rest of the week. Mr. Miller is getting you that proposal in the next hour and Mr. Tucker should be calling at one. I've already ordered your usual lunch and it will arrive at noon. Is there anything else I can do for you?" She asks sweetly as she tucks her hands behind her back.

The movement tests the strength of her buttons and for the millionth time in the last four months, I wish that I could ask her out to dinner.

"No. Thank you," I say shortly and Noel's smile dims slightly.

I want to punch myself in the face when I see her eyes turn downward.

"What are your lunch plans?" I ask her, desperate to bring her smile back.

"I was going to sneak out and head to that Red Line Diner. There's this hot chocolate brand that I absolutely love and they're the only ones in town who sell it."

She babbles about what she's going to order for lunch and more about the hot chocolate and how good it is. I make a mental reminder to find out the brand and make sure we always have it in stock in our break room.

"That sounds good," I say when she's finished and she groans.

"Oh, it's so good," she says that bright grin back on her face and my heart flips over in my chest.

"Maybe I'll join you for lunch," I say before I can stop myself and I expect Noel to get awkward and make up some excuse, but she shocks me by clapping her hands in excitement.

"That would be great! It always gets lonely eating lunch by myself."

"Well if you ever want company, just let me know," I tell her and for a second I think that she's going to hug me.

"I'll go cancel your usual lunch," she says as she rushes out of my office and back to her desk.

She bends over, digging around in the top drawer for something and my eyes zero in on her round ass.

"Fuck," I whisper, closing my eyes as my cock comes roaring back to life inside my pants.

How am I going to make it through lunch without pulling her onto the table and eating her instead?

TWO

Noel

I TRY NOT to be too obvious as I watch Mason under my eyelashes. He's sitting across the booth from me, his blue eyes taking in the old diner.

He doesn't look impressed.

He never really shows emotion though. Not around me anyway. He keeps it all buckled up, his face a blank mask, whenever I'm nearby.

It drives me crazy.

I feel like he's hiding something from me and it's been driving me crazy ever since I started to work for him.

I can still remember the first time that I laid eyes on Mason Roth. I was teetering in some brand new high heels, nervous as hell as I waited for my interview. There were twelve other candidates in the waiting room with me and I watched as one beautiful woman after another walked into his office and then stormed out a few minutes later.

I had heard the rumors that Mr. Roth was a domineering asshole and normally, I wouldn't have applied to work for someone like that, but I was desperate. My roommate was moving out and I either needed to find a higher paying job or somehow find a new roommate in the next two days.

When my name was called, I stood on shaky legs and took a deep breath before I made my way inside his palatial office. He was seated behind his desk like a king and I had hurried across the space and shoved my hand out over his desk.

He had looked up, his blue eyes meeting mine and widening imperceptibly. We're both silent for a minute as I wait for him to take my offered hand.

"I'm Noel Merrybell," I said, pasting a wide smile on my face.

That's always been my motto. Kill them with kindness.

Mason finally took my hand, shaking it once before he just held my hand. It had felt intimate and I remember my breath catching in my throat. He had let go of my hand, taking my resume and glancing at it cursorily.

When he set it aside a minute later, I thought for sure that I was on my way out. He had surprised me though by telling me I started immediately.

The next thing I knew I was walking back out and telling the other candidates that the position had been filled. I spent the rest of the day filling out paperwork in Mr. Roth's office. I thought I talked too much but Mason seemed to like it. He had sat behind his desk watching me, his eyes thoughtful.

I told him about studying business in college and my last job working as a receptionist for a department store downtown. I told him about growing up in Chicago with two workaholic parents and about always wanting to move to New York.

When I had told him that I was leaving my other job because I couldn't afford rent, he said that the assistant position came with an apartment. Moving trucks were at my place the next day and I was moved into my new fancy apartment by the weekend.

That was four months ago now and my crush on Mr. Roth has only grown with each passing second that I spend with him.

"What will it be?" The waitress asks as she stops at our booth and I rattle off my order.

"I'll have the same, but with a water instead of a hot chocolate," Mason says and I can't stop the gasp that spills from my mouth.

"No hot chocolate? But it's the best!" I exclaim and Mason looks at me, surprised.

"I'll take the hot chocolate too," he says quietly and the waitress nods before she turns to put our order in.

"You won't be disappointed," I say, smiling at Mason as we both lean back in the booth.

"What's so great about it?" He asks as he straightens out his silverware on his napkin.

"It's just good. I don't know what they use but it's the best. And you can only get it here," I say.

"Hmm, Mason says.

Our waitress is back a second later, sliding two hot chocolates and a water in front of us. I smile and thank her, pulling my cup closer to me and taking a big sip. I moan, closing my eyes as I sink back in my seat.

"So good," I whisper.

I hear a strangled sound and my eyes spring open to see

Mason staring at me hungrily. His eyes are so dark, his face flushed and I swear he licks his lips as he stares at me.

I don't know what comes over me but I want to keep that look on his face. I take another sip, holding his eyes with mine. When I pull the cup away, I swallow and then slowly lick my lips.

Mason swallows hard, his eyes heating even more and I feel and answering fire start deep in my belly. Maybe this crush isn't so one sided after all.

THREE

Mason

THERE ARE a few reasons why I never made a move on Noel. Sure, she works for me and things could get messy between us if our relationship went sour but it's more than that.

If I were to get a taste of Noel, I know that I would never be able to let her go. I'm already obsessed with her. There's no way I could be with her and not grow more consumed by her.

There's one last reason.

Noel deserves better than me.

My tastes are darker. I want to dominate Noel. I want her beneath me, letting me own her body. I want her on her knees, her lips wrapped tight around my cock as she deepthroats me. I want her choking and gagging on it.

Noel is too pure, too sweet for that. She is light and happy. She deserves to be treated like a queen both in and out of the bedroom. I'm sure my tastes would scare her. She's probably used to dim bedrooms lit only by candles, rose petals on silk sheets and all that.

My fingers tighten around the arms of my desk chair as I try to scrub the thought of Noel with another man from my mind. It's almost time to leave and I look out, watching as Noel starts to gather up all of her belongings.

I lean back in my chair, closing my eyes as I try to get myself under control. I already know what will happen when it's time to leave. I'll follow her home, from a distance of course. She'll go to the floor below mine and I'll head up to the penthouse and turn on the cameras that I had installed in her apartment before she moved in.

I'll spend the rest of the night watching her and jerking off until my cock finally goes down. It won't satisfy me though. I'll spend all night dreaming of Noel and wake up to thoughts of her.

I've never been attracted to women. For a long time I thought that there was something wrong with me. I've been in New York all my life, seen models and actresses and a million other beautiful women and none of them have elicited the response in me that Noel does. None of them turns me on or has me half as crazed as Noel.

She's my only. She's my future and my end.

"I'm heading out, Mr. Roth," Noel says, a bright smile aimed at me as she hitches her purse higher on her shoulder.

"It's cold out. Let Jason drive you home."

"Oh, that's alright. I'm not far."

"I don't want you catching a cold, Noel. Let him drive you."

I'm already on the phone, texting my driver and letting him know that she'll be out front in a few minutes.

"What about you?" Noel asks and I glance up to see her standing just inside the doorway,

"What about me?" I ask, confused.

"How will you get home? Aren't you leaving now too?"

"Yeah, I can grab a cab. Don't worry about me."

"I can't steal your ride. Maybe we can share?" She offers and I can't pass on the opportunity to spend time with her in an enclosed area.

I know that I'm torturing myself. Noel has shown zero interest in me in that way and she probably never will, but I just can't seem to help myself.

"Alright, give me just a minute."

I stand as Noel heads out to her desk to wait for me. I grab my coat and briefcase and meet her by the elevator. Noel chats with me about my schedule for the rest of the week and her plans for the holiday season. I'm pleased to hear that she's staying in New York for Christmas and the New Year.

I hold the car door open for Noel and slip in behind her. Noel has a bright red knit hat over her pale hair and paired with her green pea coat, she looks like a Christmas angel. There's a bite to the air and I frown, eyeing her coat. It doesn't look warm enough and I make a note to order her something warmer when I get home. She'll need mittens or gloves too and maybe a scarf.

We pull up outside our building and I debate if I should follow her inside now or ask Jason to do a lap around the building. When I hired her, I said that this place was company apartments so maybe it wouldn't look odd that I lived here too.

"This is me," Noel says and I climb out after her.

"Me too," I say as I head inside and lead her over to the elevator.

I hit her floor number and then insert my code for the penthouse.

"I forget that you live here! How come I never see you around?" Noel asks as the elevator slows and comes to a stop on her floor.

"Just stick to myself I guess," I say as the doors open and Noel steps out.

"I'll see you tomorrow morning," she says as she waves and starts to head down the hallway to her apartment.

"I'll meet you out front at 8:45. It's supposed to snow tonight and I don't want you walking in the cold," I call as the doors start to slide closed.

Noel grins and waves at me and I lean against the back wall, impatiently waiting for the elevator to reach my floor. The doors slide open and I'm in the living room, turning on the cameras a minute later.

She's inside, humming Christmas carols as she moves around her kitchen. I sink down onto the couch, smiling as I watch her start to take out pans and make something to eat. I should be doing the same but I can't seem to tear my eyes away from the screen.

I pull my phone out while she puts the pan in the oven and bring up a new browser. I order Noel a new puffy jacket and a long down one along with some new mittens and gloves and a few scarfs. I pause when I see the slippers. There are reindeer ones and before I can second guess it, I add that to my cart too. A few more knit hats and I hit checkout.

Noel is just sitting down to eat then and I grab some leftovers that my housekeeper left and sit down on the couch. I like to pretend that we're eating together. I pace myself with her so that we finish at the same time and I get up to put my empty dishes in the sink at the same time as her.

Noel heads into her bedroom and I know that she'll be there for the rest of the night. She likes to shower and read before she goes to bed. I didn't put cameras in her bedroom, just the living room and kitchen. I might be obsessed but I know that there are boundaries that I shouldn't cross.

I turn off the TV and head into my bedroom, crossing to the bathroom and stripping off my clothes. I turn the water on, cranking it so that it's almost scalding before I step under the spray.

Noel is probably showering right now too and I fantasize that she's in here with me instead of her own shower. I take my cock in hand, stroking the hot length as the water rushes over me.

I fist myself, gripping tightly as I set up a punishing rhythm. My head tips back and my eyes fall closed as I picture Noel before me. Her skin is wet and soapy, and her hands cup her heavy tits, rolling the nipples as she leans back against the shower wall.

She beckons me closer, spreading her creamy thighs open in invitation and I picture pinning her against the wall. I'll thrust into her slick channel, forcing her up onto her tiptoes as I pummel into her. Her cries would echo off the walls, driving me wild.

I come then, thick ropes of semen shooting out and landing on the shower floor. I watch as it swirls down the drain as I catch my breath. I shower and rinse off quickly before I head into my bedroom to get ready for bed. I pull on a pair of pajama pants and grab my phone as I fall back into bed.

I pull up my emails, smiling when I see the new one from one of my investment managers. The hot chocolate company that Noel loves so much is about to go out of business so I bought it instead. I don't know shit about hot chocolate but if it makes Noel happy, I would gladly spend all of my money making sure that she has it.

I plug my phone in and crawl under the covers, letting dreams of Noel and I together lull me to sleep.

FOUR

Noel

I COULD BARELY SLEEP last night. I don't know what's changed between us but I can't stop thinking about Mason. I've always had a thing for him, been attracted to him, but I've always been able to push him from my mind and concentrate on other things when I needed to. All day yesterday though, it was like he was all I could think about, all I could see.

It apparently isn't going to be better today.

I'm waiting in the lobby for Mason, my coat and hat on as I stare outside at the snow gently falling. It's only 8:30 so I know that I'm early but I was too excited to see him to stay in my apartment for another minute. When the elevator doors open a minute later and Mason steps out, I realize that maybe I wasn't the only one over excited to see the other.

"Morning!" I say cheerily as Mason joins me and together, we head toward the front door.

His car is already waiting out front and he opens the door, letting me slide in first before he joins me. Traffic is bad with the snow starting to cover the roads and it takes over half an hour for us to get to work. We go over a few of the things on his schedule for this week on the ride and I bring up that we still need to hire someone to do the annual Christmas party and to decorate around the office.

Mason leads me up to the top floor of our building and leaves me at my desk. I get situated and am just about to go get him his coffee when he appears beside me.

"Here, you can use this to get the decorations," he says as he hands me a black credit card and then disappears back into his office.

I practically skip to the break room and grab Mason his coffee. I'm about to leave when a familiar red and green logo catches my eyes. I pause and reach into the cabinet with the coffee pods, pulling out the box of hot chocolate. This wasn't here yesterday and I wonder how Mason was able to find a box when I've scoured the city and come up empty handed.

I turn back to the office and see Mason pacing in his office. He's on his phone, arguing with whoever he is talking to about something. I smile and make myself a cup of hot chocolate before I head back to my desk. I set my cup down and push into Mason's office with his cup of coffee.

His old assistant had warned me to never enter his office without knocking. Apparently, he yelled at her a time or two over that. I had been terrified when I first walked in without knocking, bracing for him to rip into me but it never came. When I had apologized, he had said that I am welcome anywhere, at any time.

I smile at him, setting his coffee on his desk as he ends his phone call.

"Thanks for the hot chocolate," I say as he takes a seat behind his desk.

"You're welcome," he says like it was no big deal but I know that he must have had to search the entire state for it.

"Anything that I can help with?" I ask, motioning to the phone.

"No, it's a business thing. One of the project managers will handle it."

I watch as he picks up his coffee and takes a sip.

"Anything that you wanted in particular for the decorations?" I ask, trying to strike up a conversation.

My days are pretty slow here, especially over the holidays. It can get boring just sitting at my desk all day.

"Whatever you like. I'm sure you have a better eye for it than me." He says and I turn to head out before I remember to ask about his lunch order.

I spin back around and I could swear that his eyes are checking out my ass. His blue ones meet my green before I can be sure though and I stumble slightly in my heels.

"Did you want your regular lunch order? Or did you want to join me for lunch again?" I ask, crossing my fingers behind my back as I wait for him to answer.

I want him to say that he'll eat with me. Yesterday was incredible, getting to spend time with him, getting to talk to him. This city can be lonely. I mean I live alone now and I work up here on this floor where it's just Mason and me.

"I'll eat with you. Did you want to go out again or order in?" He asks as his phone starts to ring. He ignores it and I smile. I like having his attention focused solely on me.

"Can we go out? I can pick up some of the decorations then too."

"Whatever you want," Mason says and I try to contain my grin.

"Alright, let me know if you need anything," I say as I head back to my desk.

I answer the phone and emails for the next few hours, counting down the seconds until it's lunch time. When 11:55 am rolls around, I go to the bathroom to freshen up before I meet Mason by the elevators and a shiver rolls through me when he places his hand on my lower back for just a second as we enter the elevator and start to head down to the first floor.

"Do you mind if we walk? The department store isn't far and we can just find someplace close by to grab lunch?" I ask him and he frowns down at my coat.

"Are you sure you're not going to be too cold?"

"I'll be fine," I tell him, pushing out the front door.

Snow is still falling lightly and I wrap my arms around my waist, bracing against the chill.

"Come here," Mason says, sounding grumpy but when he wraps his arm around me and tugs me into his side, he's gentle.

I lean against him, breathing in his cologne. I smile when I realize it's the one that I bought him for his birthday last month.

We head down the sidewalk, walking the two blocks to the department store. About half a block away, I freeze and Mason comes up short next to me.

"What?" He asks, looking around for what could have caught my attention.

"The Christmas trees! Aren't they so pretty with the snow covering their branches like that?" I ask as I step out of the way of the sidewalk traffic and into the little Christmas tree lot.

An older man approaches us, his cheeks a bright red

from the cold. He smiles as he makes his way over to us and extends his hand.

"Hey there, I'm Frank Ocher. Are you two looking for a tree?"

"I am. I need one for my apartment," I say when Mason gives me a surprised look.

"Well you're in luck! I've got a couple of different types."

Mason humors me and we follow Frank around the lot as he shows us some Douglas Firs and a few pine trees.

"This is actually my last Christmas season. I'm retiring and moving down south to be closer to my grandkids."

"What's going to happen to the Christmas tree farm?" I ask as we head back to the front of the lot.

"I'm not sure. I hope I can find someone to buy it and continue to run it but that's been tough," he says with a sigh.

I frown, looking around the lot. It makes me sad to see this place disappear. I've always loved Christmas and I wish that I had the money to buy the lot and save the trees. It's got to be a cool job selling trees and getting to spread Christmas cheer every year.

"I'll buy it," Mason blurts out and I jerk in his hold.

"Really?" Frank asks, looking just as shocked as I feel.

"Yeah. It seems a shame to have to shut down something that makes people happy."

Frank is all excited now, thanking Mason, but all I can think about is the way he had looked right at me when he said that it makes people happy.

FIVE

Mason

WHAT THE HELL am I going to do with a Christmas tree farm?

I don't know the first thing about trees or selling them but I couldn't stand to see that sad look in Noel's eyes. She was so happy when I said I would buy it. I'll never forget the smile she gave me when I promised Frank that I would take good care of his farm. That smile was worth whatever headache this Christmas tree farm will bring me.

Before I know it, I'm shaking the man's hand and he's promising to drop off a tree to Noel tonight on his way home. I text our doorman to let him know to expect a tree tonight as I lead Noel to the department store.

We head to customer service and pick up the decorations that Noel had ordered this morning. I take the bags from her and wrap my arm around her shoulder as we head back out into the cold.

We swing by a deli on the way back to the office and

grab some soup and sandwiches before we head back to the office. I hate to stop touching her but I know that once we're inside, I don't have the cold as an excuse anymore.

I dump the food and decorations on the little coffee table in my office and motion for Noel to take a seat on the sofa. She starts to unpackage our food and I hang up our coats before I join her.

I try to keep some distance between us so that Noel can't tell that the thing that I want to be eating is her. I take a bite of my sandwich, grabbing a napkin. I pass one to Noel and she thanks me. We eat in silence for a few minutes and I tense for a second when Noel tucks her leg underneath her. The move brings her closer to me on the sofa and also hikes her skirt up another inch.

Her knee presses against mine and I swear my heart tries to beat out of my chest. I look to her, trying to see if she's aware that she's touching me but she's busy eating her lunch.

"Want to help me set up the decorations after lunch?" She asks me and even though I have four new business investments to look through, I find myself nodding.

Noel smiles, her green eyes twinkling, at my answer and I feel lighter. Noel talks about the party planner that she hired for the other floors. When I found out that it was a man, I had demanded that he not do our floor.

We finish up our lunch and Noel reaches over, taking my empty soup cup from my hands. Her fingers brush against mine and seem to linger. I look up into her face but she's busy humming under her breath as she cleans up.

Is she trying to drive me crazy?

I help Noel unbox all of the decorations and we spend the next two hours hanging up tinsel and wreaths. I insist on climbing up on the chair to hang everything. I'm not going to let my girl get hurt while I just stand by.

Noel keeps touching me. At first, I thought she was trying to steady me but her hands would linger, or she would hold onto my leg when I wasn't in any danger of wobbling. With each press of her hand against my body, my cock grows harder. By the time that we're done hanging up everything, my cock has the zipper of my pants imprinted on it.

Noel helps me pick up the trash and I move to throw it out. I'm headed back to my desk when I catch Noel standing on the chair in my office. She's hanging something up on the ceiling over the door and I rush forward to make sure that she doesn't fall.

"I would have gotten that," I tell her as I hold onto her curvy hips.

I look up to see what she's hanging up and my mouth dries up when I see the small sprig of Mistletoe hanging between us. My whole body heats and I lock eyes with Noel.

"Noel, are you flirting with me?"

"So what if I am?" She whispers, her own eyes heating as she steps closer to me.

"Do you know what you're doing? You're playing a dangerous game," I whisper, my hands tightening on her hips.

"I think you might be worth it," she whispers and those words seal her fate.

I've got her off the chair and in my arms in the next second. There's still a chance that someone could come up to our floor and catch us so I back her up against my desk and hit the button for the frosted glass and the automatic locks.

"Last chance, Noel. You can walk out now and I'll let you go. But if you stay... If you stay, I'm never letting you leave. You'll be mine forever. My obsession, my future, my fucking everything. So, what's it going to be?"

My breath stalls in my lungs as she looks up into my eyes.

"I'm yours."

My lips are on hers a heartbeat later.

SIX

Noel

HIS LIPS MOLD to mine in a possessing brand. He tastes like warmth and I moan as his mouth goes to battle with mine. It feels like he's trying to mold to me, to conquer me, and I gladly bend to his will.

My hands cling to his shoulders, holding on tight so that I don't get swept away in the storm that is Mason Roth. His hands tangle in my hair, jerking my head back so that he can shove his tongue farther into my mouth.

He tongues me thoroughly, tracing every recess of my mouth as if he's trying to memorize everything about me. His other hand traces down my spine, pressing me closer against him as he starts to walk me backwards.

I bump into the wall near the bathroom and I pull away, gasping as Mason's hand dips lower and he grips my ass tightly. He presses against me, rocking me against the hard ridge in his pants. My own hips start to rock against him, grinding hard along his cock, and he presses me harder against the doorframe.

His tongue traces a path down my neck and he bites down lightly where my neck and shoulder meet. Explosions start to go off all over my body and I rub my hands over his chest, trying to touch all of him at once.

I want to come so bad— No. I need to come so bad.

My breasts feel heavy and achy inside my bra and I shift, rubbing them shamelessly against his chest.

"Does my girl need something more?" He asks, his voice husky.

"Yes," I gasp out, my blood heating as I look into Mason's eyes and see the fire burning in their depths. A fire that is all for me.

His lips claim mine once more and he pulls me away from the doorframe and pushes me into the bathroom. I'm not sure when he turned the lights on or when he pushed me over to the bathroom counter but soon his lips are gone and I'm being spun around.

I look up into the mirror, my eyes meeting Mason's. His hips pin mine to the bathroom counter and I whine low in my throat as his thigh works its way between my legs. I'm so wet that I'd be surprised if there wasn't already a wet spot on his pants.

"You need me?" He purrs, his hand wrapping around my throat and forcing me to meet his eyes in the mirror. "You walk around driving me crazy in these tight skirts. You keep taunting me and teasing me. Well, I can't take it any longer."

I gasp as his hand leaves my throat and trails roughly over my breasts. He pulls at the fabric of my shirt, ripping it out from where it was tucked into my skirt and pulling it in one motion over my head. I've barely blinked my eyes open before he's got my skirt in a puddle at my feet.

His eyes blaze, a fire igniting deep within their depths as he takes me in. I can feel the hard ridge of him swell against my ass and I moan, grinding myself back against him. His fingers tangle in my hair, wrapping around his fist and he jerks my head back.

"None of that. I'm in charge here. You'll take what I give you."

My mouth opens on a soundless cry, my eyes going blank as his words cause a fire to start deep in my womb.

"I need —"

"I know what you need," he says, cutting me off.

My nipples tighten painfully against the fabric of my bra and I reach up, needing to touch them, to ease the ache.

"Tsk, tsk," he whispers in my ear, dragging my hands back.

He undoes my bra in one smooth motion and drags the straps down my arms before he binds my wrists behind my back with it. The new position causes my back to arch, thrusting my pointed nipples high into the air. My body heats more when I see the way that his eyes are devouring me.

"So pretty," he murmurs as he drags his hands down my shoulders to cup my breasts.

I whimper at the feather light contact, needing more. I'm afraid if I say anything though, that he'll stop.

I shift in my heels, my eyes begging his and he grins back at me in the mirror.

"You want to beg me?"

"Please. Please fuck me," I almost sob and I'm rewarded with a tweak of my nipples.

"I think we can do better than that, Noel. You've been driving me mad for months. Do you know how many times I've had to take myself in hand in this very bathroom? With you just a few feet away."

"Fuck," I sob, the pressure inside me becoming too much.

His hands continue to trace light circles around my aching nipples and I feel like a bow drawn too tight. It feels like I could come with just the slightest breeze across them. My panties are soaked through and sticking to me and I can feel my heartbeat there. It's racing out of control, a constant drum that is driving me wild.

"I need you!" I scream, my voice coming out hoarse and a touch wild. "I need you inside me. I need you to fuck me more than I've ever needed anything," I say as I meet his eyes in the mirror.

Mason grins at me wolfishly as one of his hands leaves my breasts and he reaches down, tearing the thin cotton panties off of me with the flick of his wrist.

"You're so beautiful when you're begging for my cock," he whispers against my neck and my eyes fall closed as I feel him unzip his pants behind me.

I moan when the head of his cock lands against my ass, the sound turning frantic as he drags it between my ass cheeks, over my puckered hole. He pauses there for a second and my eyes spring open, meeting his in the mirror.

"I'll be taking you here too, Noel. One day soon, but this pussy has been starring in my fantasies for months."

Mason's cock trails lower and my breath catches in my throat when the tip of his hard cock lodges inside me. He wraps one fist in my hair again, pulling me back against him and crushing my hands between us.

"What's the magic word?" He whispers against my ear and it falls off my lips like a prayer.

"Please."

In the next instant, Mason is driving his hard length inside of me. I cry out as he takes my virginity but it's a mild sting. There and gone in the next second as my brain catches up with the way he's moving inside of me.

His hand tugs on my hair, the nerve endings in my scalp lighting up. I meet his eyes in the mirror and the look on his face takes my breath away.

He's like a man possessed.

His eyes are so dark they almost look black and his lips are drawn back as if he's in pain.

"So goddamn tight. You've been saving this pussy for me, haven't you?" He asks and I can only nod.

I'm transfixed by the way he's watching me, by the way he's taking me in. It's like I'm something priceless. Something that he fought and worked for and now he's finally getting to enjoy the spoils of his victories. He's looking at me like he's never going to let me go.

That thought almost buckles my knees and Mason lets go of my hair to grip my waist. I'm still pinned against the sink so it's not like I can go anywhere.

I love the feeling of his hands on me as he starts to rock in and out of me. The pace is great at first but soon my body has grown used to his rhythm and I know I need more. I need him to lose control and take me.

I try to rock my hips back, to meet his thrusts, but Mason's fingers just tighten on my hips.

"Don't you dare try to rush me. I've been waiting so long to feel this snug cunt wrapped around me like a fist. I'm going to savor this."

His words leave me feeling dizzy and I tighten my hands into fists behind my back. Mason's hands leave my waist, traveling up my body until they're molding my tits in his hands once more.

He pinches and toys with my nipples until I'm nothing but feeling. It's as if the only thing in the world that I care about are his hands on my breasts and his thick cock working between my thighs.

It's still not enough though.

I wiggle against Mason, desperate for more and his hand leaves my breast, wrapping around my throat. He doesn't squeeze hard, just leaves it there, letting me know that he's in charge. He slides his hand up, cupping my chin and forcing me to meet his eyes in the mirror.

"You want me to pound this pussy? To rut into you and take you like some kind of animal?"

My eyes widen and darken with lust and I know that he doesn't need me to answer that question. He can see it written all over my face.

"Beg me, Noel. You should know by now that I'm powerless to tell you no. Not when you beg."

"Please. I want to see you lose control," I gasp out and I can see the immediate change in Mason.

His eyes darken to black but a new fire seems to light inside them. It's almost like his obsession with me has finally boiled over and he can't hide it anymore.

"Yes, yes," I whisper as his hips rear back.

He plunges deep inside of me and I cry out, my body bending forward over the sink as he starts to fuck me harder.

"No," Mason growls, his hand wrapping in my hair and jerking me up. "I get to watch when you come apart all over my cock."

It almost happens then just from his words, just from the look on his face as his eyes lock on my face. They scan my features like he's committing this to memory and I stare right back.

"You know how crazy you make me? I can't concentrate. I can't think straight. Every thought I have is just you. I live to make you happy, to see you smile. You think I wanted to buy a Christmas tree farm? Or that hot chocolate company? No. They're both terrible investments but I can't seem to say no. Not when it's something that makes you smile."

I'm staring at him wide eyed, my orgasm stirring to a crescendo inside of me as he keeps talking, as his fingers and cock keep working.

"Seeing you frown makes me feel like a bastard and has me scrambling to fix it. Lord only knows what I would do if you cried."

His hand leaves my hair and he cups my face, turning my face until his lips meet mine.

"You're mine, Noel. You have been since I laid eyes on you. Say it. Say it as you come all over my cock."

"I'm yours!" I scream as I do as he asks and let my orgasm suck me under.

My body falls forward, my head and chest resting on the counter as Mason drives himself into me, once, twice, three times. He swells, his cock sinking deep as he lets go and comes deep inside of me. I can feel his warm release splash rope after rope deep inside of me and I shiver and shake as his orgasm triggers another baby one in me.

I'm panting, a sweaty sticky mess, when Mason pulls out of me and undoes my hands. He rubs my wrists, making sure that there's no marks before he spins me around and pulls me into his arms.

"I love you, Noel. I need you more than my next breath. Always."

I tip my chin up, meeting his eyes as I wrap my arms around his neck.

"I love you too."

SEVEN

Mason

SHE'S MINE. She's finally fucking mine.

As soon as those three words are past her lips, I have her bundled back in her coat and am dragging her into the elevator. It's not quite quitting time but I need to get Noel home, in my bed, beneath me again.

I text my driver and soon I'm sliding into the backseat of the town car after her. As soon as we're inside, I drag Noel into my lap and fuse our mouths together. We spend the drive home making out like teenagers. I've got my hands worked under her skirt, her legs straddling me, and I'm about to take her again when the car slows.

I bite out a curse as our apartment building comes into view. I tug her skirt back down and help her out of the car. Our doorman stops me and informs me that the tree was delivered a few minutes ago.

"Can you bring it up to my place, please," I ask him as I

lead Noel over to the elevator and punch in my code for the penthouse.

I should probably warn her about the cameras that I have in her apartment and the pictures that are hanging in my place but it seems too late now. After the bathroom, she has to have some inkling of how obsessed I am with her, of how she rules my every thought.

The elevator doors open and I take Noel's hand, leading her inside. Her eyes are wide as she takes in the entry hall and takes in the mostly empty walls. I lead her into the living room and kitchen and offer to make her something to eat.

"Can we just order pizza?" She asks, her eyes a mixture of awe and lust.

"We can do whatever you want to," I tell her and I take out my phone and order from a pizza parlor close by.

"It will be here in half an hour," I tell her and I look up to see her moving closer to me.

Her arms loop around my waist and it feels like all is right in the world.

"What are we going to do while we wait?" She asks me in a seductive whisper.

"I've got a few ideas," I say as I pull her after me down the hallway and into our bedroom.

And it is *our* bedroom now. I won't spend another night without her. Not now that I've had a taste of her.

Noel comes up short when she sees the walls. Canvases and framed photographs of her hang on every wall. She doesn't seem that upset by them. More confused, and I give her a second to adjust before I try to explain.

"I've wanted you since I first laid eyes on you. You're the only woman that I have ever had this reaction too. You're the only woman that I've ever loved or wanted. I'm so obsessed with you, Noel. Does that scare you?" I ask her, waiting anxiously for her answer.

"No, it probably should, but it doesn't. In fact, I think I like it," she says as she turns to face me.

"Thank fuck because there's no way that I could stop."

I'm about to crush her to me, about to rip every stitch of clothing off of us and pin her to the bed when there's a knock at my front door.

"Don't move," I instruct Noel as I head over to answer it.

I have to adjust myself in my pants and I bite back a curse at whoever was dumb enough to interrupt me from spending more time with Noel. I answer the door, helping the doorman drag the Christmas tree inside and over to the wall by the window.

I tip him and thank him as he steps back into the elevator and I turn and hurry into the bedroom. The sight that greets me has my cock raging back to life in my pants.

Noel is naked, spread out on the bed before me. She looks wet and ready for me to claim her and when she crooks a finger at me, giving me a saucy smirk, I let myself loose. I've stripped and crawled between her legs in the blink of the eye and Noel giggles, spreading her thighs wide as my cock pushes inside of her.

Pictures of Noel hang on the walls as I take her for the first time in our bed. I thought that once I had finally made love to her, that the need inside me would subside, at least for a bit, but that doesn't seem to be the case.

In fact, I think my need for her has only grown.

EIGHT

Noel

MASON WOKE me up with his head between my legs. I was a little sore after yesterday but it was a good kind of sore. He had eaten me to one orgasm and then another and then a third. I had been about to pass out again when he had carried me into the shower and pinned me against the wall.

I had clung to him, my fingernails scratching his back as he pounded into me. I love the way he makes love to me. I love how he takes over and I love giving up my control to him.

He had washed me in the shower afterward, his hands soft and loving as they washed me. I had let Mason take care of me, letting him wash and dry me off. I had to sneak out to head downstairs to my apartment so I could get dressed but Mason found me. Of course he did.

"You wait for me from now on. In fact, I'll have movers here today and you'll never have to leave without me again."

I should probably be worried about how fast things are

moving between us, but it feels so right. His dark side, this obsession he has with me, doesn't scare me. It thrills me. He makes me feel cherished and loved.

Maybe it's because my parents were always too busy working to pay much attention to me. Maybe that's why I'm so drawn to Mason and the way he loves me.

I get dressed and join Mason in the kitchen. He's already on the phone, talking to the movers and I roll my eyes when he says that tomorrow doesn't work. It has to be today.

I head past him to grab my peacoat out of the hallway closet but Mason stops me.

"I got you something," he says and I take his hand as he leads me back to the elevator and up to his place.

He opens the hallway closet and I'm surprised to see two new coats and some new mittens and scarves inside.

"Your other stuff wasn't warm enough," he explains as he grabs the long puffy coat and holds it out to me.

I slip my arms in and zip it up as Mason grabs me some mittens, a hat, and a scarf.

"It wasn't snowing that hard out there," I protest as Mason loops the scarf around my neck.

"It's cold though. Especially with the wind," he protests and I let him lead me back to the elevator and down to the lobby.

I wave at Trevor, the day doorman, as we head outside. I figure we must be walking today since he bundled me up so much that I'm already sweating. Mason steers me over to the waiting town car and I slide in when he opens the door for me. I tug off my hat and scarf, giggling when I see Mason frowning at my actions.

"It's so hot in here," I say as I tug off the mittens and shove them into my new coat's pocket. "Thank you for the new coat and winter gear," I add, leaning over to kiss Mason's cheek.

He tugs me onto his lap, or tries to anyway. The long coat wraps around my knees and Mason lets out a frustrated sound as he turns me sideways and cuddles me on his lap. The snow is coming down harder today and I watch the flurries out the window as I rest in Mason's arms.

"What happens now? Will I need to go to HR and sign something? Will we have to disclose our relationship or something?"

My mind races with questions as real life catches up with me. I love Mason but maybe I should be thinking about protecting myself in case things go bad between us.

"No," Mason says, burying his nose in my hair and tracing the tip of my ear.

"What do you mean no?" I ask and doubts start to push in.

"No, you don't need to sign anything. The rest of the company will know soon. You'll own half of everything soon enough."

Is he talking about marriage?

"The movers will be moving your stuff into our place today. Trevor is going to let them in," Mason asks and I wonder if he's trying to distract me.

"Maybe we can decorate the tree and your place–"

"Our place," Mason corrects and I smile, burying my face in his neck.

"Sorry, our place. Maybe we can decorate our place tonight."

"Whatever you want, Noel. Although, we will need to buy decorations because I don't have any."

"Scrooge," I tease and Mason nips my earlobe.

We pull up in front of work a minute later and I reluctantly climb out after him. He holds my hand as we head into work and I spot the looks I get from the other employees right away.

Their eyebrows shoot up and they turn, whispering to each other as we wait for the elevator to come.

Once again, doubts start to creep in. Sure, Mason is into me now but what happens if his feelings change? He's the CEO and founder of Roth Investments and he'll be fine if we break up. I'll be the one who is screwed. I'll be out of a job, an apartment, and I have a feeling that my heart will be broken beyond repair.

NINE

Mason

NOEL HAS BEEN ACTING strange all day. I had thought maybe I had scared her with my lovemaking or with moving her in so quickly but she had seemed fine this morning. She was happy, teasing me and cuddling in my lap, and then we got to work.

She had seemed tense when we got into the elevator with some other employees but she didn't say anything. I had thought maybe she was just hungry. We had gotten sidetracked this morning and I didn't have time to make her anything.

I ordered her breakfast though and she still seems quiet. It's like she's worried about something but she won't tell me what. How can I fix it if she won't tell me what's wrong?

I send her off early, letting her take the town car to the department store to pick up some more decorations. I wanted to join her but a meeting came up that I couldn't reschedule.

Part of me wonders if she just needs some time alone to process the last twenty-four hours. I'm willing to give Noel anything that she needs. If she needs a few hours to herself, then that's what she'll get but by the end of the night, she'll be in my arms, in my bed.

I leave work early and jog the few blocks home. Noel is home already, bags and boxes of decorations scattered around the living room. She's sitting in the middle of the chaos, the eye in the center of the storm.

"Hey, baby," I say, pulling her into my arms and cradling her face in my hands. "How was your afternoon?"

"Good, I found some really cute decorations," she says, starting to pull away.

I let her go reluctantly, taking a seat as she starts to show me the stuff that she got today. I pull out the pot roast that my housekeeper left us for dinner and we take a break from decorating to eat.

Noel still seems quiet and part of me starts to panic. Is she having second thoughts about us already? I'll just have to make sure that I prove to her that this is meant to be, that no one will love her more than me.

I take her hand when the last ornament is hung on the tree and lead her into the bedroom. Her eyes heat and that same spark comes back into her eyes. The one that lets me know that we're on the same page.

I take my time undressing us both, peeling the layers off so that I can worship the goddess beneath them. When we're both naked, I lay her out on the bed and bracket her body with mine.

"You're mine, Noel."

She nods, her eyes hooded as she stares up at me.

"Say it," I demand and she gives me what I want without hesitation.

"I'm yours," she says, her voice husky as her back arches and she rubs her breasts against my chest.

I give her a rough kiss, my lips claiming hers in a bruising manner. She moans against my lips and the sound goes straight to my cock. I pull my lips away from hers, licking a path down her neck. I nip her collarbone, causing her to gasp before I move lower.

My hands grasp her plump tits and I hold them up for my mouth. Noel arches into me, begging me to take the stiff peaks into my mouth. I happily oblige her, sucking one rosy nipple into my mouth and teasing the taut bud. I give the other one the same attention, switching back and forth between them until Noel is half crazed, her head thrown back on the pillow, and a rosy flush covering her body.

"Please, Mason! I need more," She yells and I nip the soft skin of her breast before I move lower.

I shove her thighs open as wide as they will go and settle between them. She's soaked, her pussy lips pink and glistening in the low light.

"Who does this belong to?" I ask, dragging my thumb between her lips.

"It's yours, Mason. It's all yours," she pants and I grin as I lean forward and part her pussy with my tongue.

I don't tease her. Instead I dive in, rubbing my face through her juices until they're coating my cheeks and chin. I suck on her clit, drawing the sensitive bundle of nerves into my mouth and rolling my tongue over it until Noel is shaking.

I shove my tongue into her snug channel, fucking her with my tongue as her thighs close tight around my ears. Her hands tunnel into my hair, holding me to her as if I would ever try to leave.

I wrap my hands around her thighs, pulling her closer to

my mouth as I feel her start to spasm and come against my face.

"Mason!" She shouts, her voice hoarse as her pussy pulses against my tongue.

I'm up her body, shoving my cock into her slick cunt and starting to rut before her orgasm can even subside.

"Say it," I demand as I wrap one hand around her throat and force her to meet my eyes. "Give me what I want."

"I'm yours, I'm yours, I'm yours," she chants, her eyes dark with lust.

I lose track of how many times I order her to tell me who she belongs to and how many times she comes before I finally find my own release. I sink in as far as I can go, making sure my balls are pressed up tight to her ass, when I finally let go.

"Noel," I breathe out, her name the only word left in my brain.

I pull out reluctantly, shifting to my side and pulling Noel into my arms. She rests her head on my chest and throws a leg over my waist as her breathing evens out and she falls asleep.

I lay awake for a long time after that, wondering why she seemed so distant today and how I can convince her that there's nowhere else for her to be but in my arms. How can I prove that no one will make her happier or love her more?

By the time the sun starts to rise, I still don't have an answer. The only thing that I know is that if I lose Noel, I will lose my mind.

And my heart.

TEN

Noel

THE NEXT MORNING starts out the same as the day before. I could get used to waking up with Mason's head between my legs. He takes me in the shower before he washes and dries me off. He makes us each a bagel while I get dressed and I let him bundle me up just like he did yesterday morning even though I know that I'll be taking it all off in the car.

It isn't until we get to work that I start to remember what was bothering me so much yesterday. I think the whispers are louder today and it feels like everyone is turning to look our way.

I try to hide my discomfort from Mason but I can tell that he knows that something is bothering me. It gets a little easier once we're on our floor and there's no one else around. I try to get lost in emails and work. Mason has back to back meetings all day and I sit in on them, taking notes.

I notice some of the managers giving me side eyed looks

when they leave the conference room and I have to excuse myself to the restroom. Things are so perfect between us when we're alone but once we're at work, I can't get those looks out of my head. I wish I knew what Mason was thinking but it seems like it would come across as clingy if I asked him. I mean, it's only been two days. He moved me in with him but was that just so it was easier to hook up? He only said he loves me that one time and it was probably just a heat of the moment thing.

I splash some cold water on my face and take a deep breath before I walk out of the bathroom. When I come out, Mason is standing there with his coat on and mine through over his arm.

"Let's head home," he says and I nod as he helps me into my coat.

He holds my hand as we get into the elevator and opens the car door for me as usual. It's five o'clock and I see the other employees openly staring at us as I slide into his car. He wouldn't flaunt our relationship like this if he wasn't serious about me. Would he?

The ride home is silent as Mason texts something on his phone and I try to sort out my thoughts. I let Mason help me out of the car and lean on him as we ride the elevator up to our place.

I don't notice it at first. Too lost in thought, I suppose. When I realize that Mason isn't following me, I turn to see what caught his attention.

He's right behind me, an intense look in his eyes and I glance around.

"What's wrong?" I ask.

He points a finger up to the ceiling and I tilt my chin up, gasping when I see that mistletoes have been attached to every square inch of the ceiling.

"Mason?" I ask, my eyes starting to fill with tears.

I look back down to see Mason on one knee in front of me.

"Noel, you're mine. At first, I was thinking that you only kissed me and this only started because of the mistletoe, and if that's the case, well then I never want you to stop. I love you, Noel. I've been so afraid to tell you how I feel and scare you off but then I saw you at work and realized that you needed me to confirm this thing between us."

He digs in his pocket, pulling out a large oval cut ring and slips it onto my finger.

"You're mine, Noel. And I'm yours. I have been since you first walked into my office. I knew then that this thing between us was real. I also knew that I was obsessed and I was worried that I would scare you off with how intense my feelings for you are but I can't hide it anymore."

Tears slide down my cheeks as I watch him rise to his feet.

"I can't lose you, Noel. If you left, you would take more than just my heart with you. You would take my sanity. You're my whole world. So, I'm not going to ask you. I can't risk the chance of you saying no and me having to kidnap you. We're getting married. We can live anywhere you want, have as many kids as you want, vacation and do whatever you want. All I want is to be by your side."

"I want that too," I choke out as I wrap my arms around his neck and bury my face in his chest. "I love you, Mason. I love you so much and I need you too. I was just worried that you were going to have second thoughts and leave me and I would be left jobless, homeless, and heartbroken."

"I'll never leave you. And you're not leaving me either," he says against the top of my head and I nod, holding him tighter.

"Deal," I say, tilting my head up and he smirks down at me.

"Kiss me," he orders and I gladly rise up on my tiptoes and press my mouth against his.

"By the way," he says, pulling away from my lips a fraction of an inch. "We're getting married by the end of the month."

I laugh against his lips, smiling.

"I wouldn't have it any other way."

ELEVEN

Mason

ONE YEAR LATER...

I LEFT WORK EARLY, anxious to get home to my wife. If I know her, she's decorating without me, even though I explicitly told her not to this morning. She doesn't need to be standing on chairs when she's six months pregnant with our first child.

We got married a week after I asked her, in a small courthouse ceremony. I flew her parents in and then took her to Paris for our honeymoon.

I nod to Trevor when he opens the door for me and punch in my code, counting down the seconds until I can have my wife in my arms, her curvy body pressed up tight against mine.

The doors open and I toss my coat and briefcase aside, heading in search of my girl. The living room is a mess, boxes and decorations scattered about but no sign of Noel. I head down the hall, poking my head into the nursery but finding it empty.

Noel wanted the sex to be a surprise and I want to make my wife happy so we painted it a soft green with light grey furniture. A few blankets sit on top of the dresser and I make a note to put them away later.

I head further down the hall, stopping outside our bedroom door when I see Noel inside. She's standing on a stool, her tongue caught between her teeth as she reaches up to hang the mistletoe to the ceiling.

I creep forward, wrapping my hands around her waist so that she doesn't fall as I press a soft kiss to her growing baby bump.

"I see you didn't listen," I say as I help Noel down from the stool.

"Yeah, maybe I should be punished," she says, looking up at me from beneath her lashes.

We haven't been having as intense love making sessions as usual. I've been worried about hurting her or the baby ever since her bump started to show. At first, Noel seemed to enjoy the softer lovemaking but lately, she's been dropping hints that she wants something harder, something rougher.

"How would you like to be punished?" I ask as I walk her back toward the bed.

She surprises me by ducking under my arm when we reach the bed and pushing me down instead.

"I want to suck your cock and then have you take me from behind. I want you to pull my hair and spank me while you ride me hard," she purrs and my cock rises to the challenge.

"Whatever you want," I say as Noel undoes my buckle.

I lift my hips, helping her pull my pants and boxers off. Noel kneels between my legs, her small hands wrapping around my shaft and pumping as a pearl of come forms on the tip. She leans forward, slurping up the drop and I groan as another one replaces it.

Noel wraps her lips around me, stuffing as much of my dick into her mouth as she can and sucking. She gags slightly as she tries to deep throat me and I groan, tipping my head up and doing my best not to spill down her throat so soon.

Her hands find my balls and she rolls them gently in her palms as she continues to choke and gag along my cock. I can feel my orgasm starting, the familiar tingles going off at the base of my spine and before I can blow, I reach down and drag Noel up.

I've got her on her hands and knees, my hand fisted in her hair as I plow into her from behind in the next second.

"Fuck," I hiss as I sink balls deep into her soft cunt.

"Harder!" She begs and just like always, I'm powerless to do anything but what my wife wants.

I can feel her pussy starting to spasm around my length, her walls trying to massage the come from my balls and when she finally goes over the edge, she takes me with her. I help her lay down on her side, spooning behind her as my fingers go to her lower back, rubbing soothing circles there.

"Hmm," Noel hums. "Have I told you how much I love you?" She asks sleepily and I kiss her shoulder as I smile.

"Not this hour."

"I love you," she says instantly and I trail more kisses over her shoulder and up her neck.

"I love you more," I whisper in her ear.

TWELVE

Noel

I JUST DROPPED the kids off at school and I should probably be going home. We're headed to Chicago tonight to spend Christmas with my parents and I still have to pack for everyone but I can't resist this chance. We're going to be with parents and kids for the next week and that means no real chances to make love.

Roger, my driver, drops me off outside Mason's building and I thank him, letting him know that I'll message him when I'm ready to be picked up.

Security lets me through and I hurry over to the elevator. I have a feeling that security is already calling my husband and letting him know that I'm here. They're going to ruin my surprise but I know that they're just doing their job.

The doors open on the top floor and I can't stop the laugh when I see my husband standing there waiting for me.

"Mr. Roth, you have a meeting in fifteen minutes," Brent, his new assistant, reminds him before he looks up and sees me standing there. "Mrs. Roth, lovely to see you again," he says with a warm smile and I return it.

"You too, Brent. I hope he isn't working you too hard," I say as Mason drags me into the office, closing and locking the door behind us.

The windows are frosted a second later and I'm being pushed up against the nearest wall a heartbeat after that. We've made love on every surface in the office over the last five years.

"What are you doing here, Mrs. Roth?" Mason asks in my ear and I grin up at him mischievously.

"We're about to be trapped in a house with our kids and my parents for a week. I need my Mason fix," I say as I start to pull at his clothes.

"Oh, Noel. You know that I'm going to find every available opportunity to get you alone while we're in Chicago. I already talked to your parents and they're going to babysit so we can have a date night while we're home. I already booked the hotel," he says as his mouth traces kisses down my neck.

"Oh, then I guess I can go home," I tease, grinning when Mason's fingers tighten on my hips.

"Since you're already here," he says, trailing off as he pulls my sweater over my head and goes to work on my pants.

"What about your meeting?" I ask, kicking off my shoes.

"They can wait. The whole world can wait until after I've made my wife happy."

He lifts me into his arms, slowly lowering me down onto his length and we both moan as I clench around him.

"Love you, Mason," I breathe out as he starts to move me up and down his thick length.

"Love you more, Noel," Mason says before his lips land on mine and we get lost in each other.

Just like always.

AFTERWORD

The Warming Up to Love authors have teamed up to bring you nine new romances guaranteed to chase away the winter chill. We hope you have a wonderful holiday season filled with joy, love, and hot book boyfriends & get ready to be warmed up to love!

Hugs and KISSES,
The Warming Up to Love Authors

Check out all the Warming Up to Love books!

Snowy Kisses by Elisa Leigh
Winter Kisses by Flora Ferrari
Unwrapped Kisses by Jenna Rose
Warm Kisses by Loni Ree
Naughty Kisses by Mayra Statham
Sugar Kisses by Megan Wade
Christmas Kisses by Mila Crawford & Aria Cole
Holly Kisses by Penelope Wylde
Mistletoe Kisses by Shaw Hart

ABOUT THE AUTHOR

If you enjoyed this story, please consider leaving a review on Amazon or any other reader site or blog that you like. Don't forget to recommend it to your other reader friends.

If you want to chat with me, please consider joining my VIP list or connecting with me on one of my Social Media platforms. I love talking with each of my readers. Links below!

Website
Newsletter

His New Year Resolution

Remembering Valentine's Day

Finding Their Rhythm

Her Scottish Savior

Stealing Her

Hop Stuff

Dream Boat

Series by Shaw Hart

Telltale Heart Series

Bought and Paid For

His Miracle

Pretty Girl

Ash Mountain Pack Series

Growling For My Mate

Claiming My Mate

Mated For Life

Chasing My Mate

Protecting Our Mate

Love Note Series

Signing Off With Love

Care Package Love

Wrong Number, Right Love

Folklore Series

Kidnapped by Bigfoot

Loved by Yeti

Claimed by Her Sasquatch

Rescued by His Mermaid

Chasing Her Unicorn

Eye Candy Ink Series

Atlas

Mischa

Sam

Zeke

Nico

www.ingramcontent.com/pod-product-compliance
Lightning Source LLC
Chambersburg PA
CBHW021759150726
47989CB00004B/1714